JE
MAY

Farber, Erica.
Pirate soup

MERCER MAYER'S
CRITTERS OF THE NIGHT™
PIRATE SOUP

Written by Erica Farber and J. R. Sansevere

A Random House PICTUREBACK® Shape Book
Random House 🏠 New York

Copyright © 1996 Big Tuna Trading Company, LLC.
CRITTERS OF THE NIGHT™ is a trademark of Big Tuna Trading Company, LLC.
All rights reserved under International and Pan-American Copyright Conventions.
Published in the United States by Random House, Inc., New York, and
simultaneously in Canada by Random House of Canada Limited, Toronto.
Library of Congress Catalog Card Number: 95-74998   ISBN 0-679-87364-3
Printed in the United States of America   10 9 8 7 6 5 4 3

 A BIG TUNA TRADING COMPANY, LLC/J. R. SANSEVERE BOOK

I jumped out of bed
without making a sound.
I grabbed my pirate-
fighting things.

Quietly, I crept out of the house.
I got my trusty dinghy
and pulled it down to the water.
Then what did I do?

I rowed out to sea—
right up to the pirate ship.

There, in the middle of the deck,
stood a mean old pirate
with a big sharp sword
and a pistol in his belt.
So what did I do?

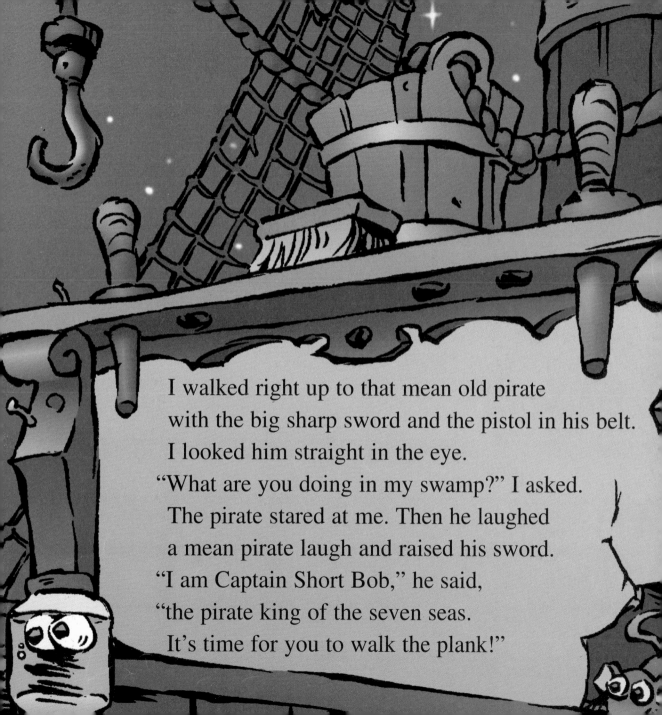

I walked right up to that mean old pirate
with the big sharp sword and the pistol in his belt.
I looked him straight in the eye.
"What are you doing in my swamp?" I asked.
The pirate stared at me. Then he laughed
a mean pirate laugh and raised his sword.
"I am Captain Short Bob," he said,
"the pirate king of the seven seas.
It's time for you to walk the plank!"

The other pirates laughed.
Then one of them blindfolded me
and shoved me onto the plank.
"Walk, boy!" shouted Captain Short Bob.
So what did I do?

I pulled out some of my pirate-fighting things.
"Do you want some bubble gum?" I asked the pirates.
"Yum-yum!" they yelled.
So I gave them each a piece of gum.

Captain Short Bob blew a big bubble.
But I blew a bigger bubble.
The other pirates cheered.
And that mean old pirate captain
got mad again.
"Time for you to walk the plank!" he said.
So what did I do?

I pulled out some more pirate-fighting things.

"Do you want to play checkers?" I said.

"Only if I can be red," said the captain.

So the captain and I played checkers.

I let him win the first game.

Then I won the second.

The pirates cheered again.

The captain got mad again.

"To the plank!" he shouted.

So what did I do?

It was time to use my best pirate-fighting thing.
"Come to my house for some pirate soup," I said.
"You make pirate soup?" Captain Short Bob sneered.
"Yes, I do," I said. "The best pirate soup on the seven seas!"

Pirate soup is made of peanut butter and chocolate
and marshmallows and onions and cherry soda.
Captain Short Bob eyed my kettle.
"Taste it!" I told the captain.
The captain scowled. Then I put a big spoonful in his mouth.
"This is really good pirate soup," he said.

After all the soup was gone,
Captain Short Bob wanted to dance.
Pirates love to dance. So we did a jig.
Then all the pirates got tired.
So what did I do?

I put the pirates to bed.
I let them sleep in my room with me.

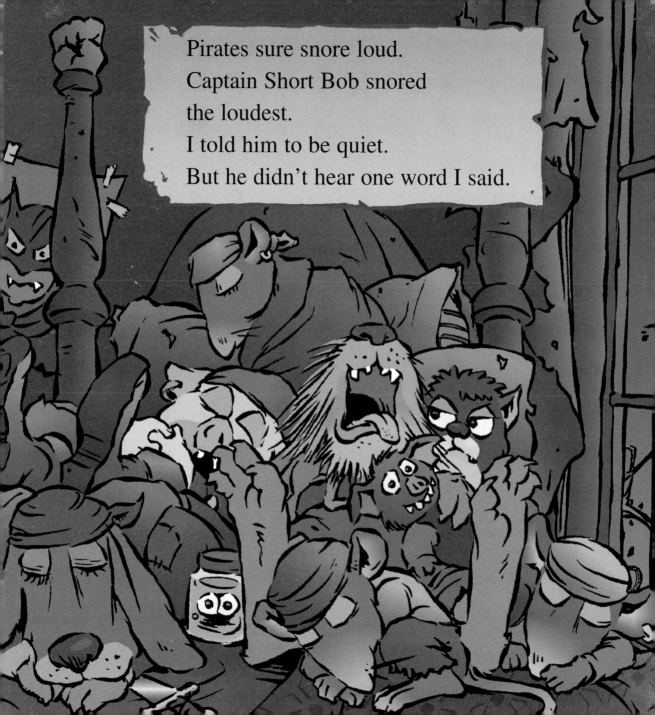

Pirates sure snore loud.
Captain Short Bob snored
the loudest.
I told him to be quiet.
But he didn't hear one word I said.

So, if you ever see a pirate ship outside your window, now you know what to do!